A CONCEPTION OF LOVE

A CONCEPTION OF LOVE

a play by Francis Warner

I see men as trees, walking.

MARK, 8:24.

OXFORD THEATRE TEXTS 5

COLIN SMYTHE, GERRARDS CROSS, 1978

British Library Cataloguing in Publication Data

Warner, Francis
A conception of love – (Oxford theatre texts;
5; 0141-1152).
I. Title
822'.9'14   PR6073.A724C/

ISBN 0-86140-005-4
ISBN 0-86140-006-2 Pbk.

First published in 1978 by Colin Smythe Ltd
Gerrards Cross, Buckinghamshire

Distributed in N. America by Humanities Press Inc
171 First Avenue, Atlantic Highlands,
N.J. 07716, U.S.A.

Photographs and cover design by
Billett Potter of Oxford

Femmes arbres 1937 by Paul Delvaux

Printed in England
by Billing & Sons Ltd, Guildford, Worcester
and London

FOR ROSALIND

A CONCEPTION OF LOVE was commissioned by the Oxford
University Experimental Theatre Club for the *Observer Oxford
Festival of Theatre* 1978, and was first performed in the Burton
Rooms of the Oxford Playhouse on Thursday, May 4th 1978. It
was directed by the author. The closing dance was arranged by
Jacki Kiers and Ruth Green.

The cast was as follows:

Griot	*John Collinson*
Broomy	*Richard Goolden*
Thalassios	*Nigel Le Vaillant*
Gan	*William Wood*
Fashshar	*Colin Burnie*
Koinonia	*Stella Hartley*
Amatrix	*Rosalind Jeffrey*
Mara	*Margie Nalty*

Characters

Griot	*the Master of an Oxford college*
Broomy	*the college gardener*
Thalassios	*an undergraduate*
Gan	*an undergraduate, his friend*
Fashshar	*a young don*
Koinonia	*an undergraduate*
Amatrix	*an undergraduate, her friend*
Mara	*a woman from London*

The play is set in Oxford.

There are two Acts.

Note
The original production was played in the round, with actors and actresses sitting among the audience.

The relationship of the cast to garden trees was indicated in the opening scene by Broomy addressing Griot as the ailanthus, pointing to Fashshar in the distance as the cedar, and speaking of Mara as the tulip tree, Koinonia as the maidenhair, Amatrix as the chestnut, Thalassios as the ilex, and Gan as the hornbeam.

All the characters are fictitious.

Act One

Broomy with besom, sweeping.
Enter to him Griot, informally dressed.

BROOMY   Morning, Master of the College.

GRIOT   Morning, Broomy. After all these years you still never use my name.

BROOMY   Funny French one; can't get my mouth round it. If you don't mind me asking, sir : what does it mean?

GRIOT   Griot? Oh, it's probably African originally, though remains of the French occupation still cling round it. The griot is the story-teller of the tribe; he perpetuates its beliefs and customs – though that's going back a long way.

BROOMY   Sort of priest, you might say? I go back a long way, too. I well remember your late wife, God bless her! Always called her Mrs Master. She was a lovely woman. Your children grown up and gone, too. I remember them when you first came to this College. Teenagers they were then.

GRIOT   They marry and make their homes, and I get my grandchildren.

BROOMY   Eh, hey! That's what it's all about. Now I love my
              trees here; naming them, talking to them winter
              and summer. The young come and go, but these
              don't wander. Look at that Tree of Heaven there,
              the ailanthus, reaching up to the sky like a hand in
              a glove! Oh, my back. It fair hurts to look to the
              top sudden-like. And this old devil of a cedar, making
              wolf hand-shadows with its branches.

GRIOT   The cedar of Lebanon. Egypt means 'black' and
              Lebanon means 'white'. Strange, isn't it? But it
              probably means 'the white mountain' where all these
              cedars originate.

BROOMY   Well, there you got me, I don't know; but they say
              some's as old as Solomon, and it's the wood that
              made the Cross. Damned old tree! (*Chuckles*) Then
              there are the ladies, as I call them. (*Pause*)
              Thousands of greeny-white and yellow flowers on
              that tulip-tree all through June and July. Oh, she's
              a show-off. Look at that trunk. Here, feel it, with
              all those well-filled bulges.

GRIOT   We need her brashness in this garden.

BROOMY   And look at the lovely slender trunk of this maiden-
              hair. Unmarked. Just a touch of moss for colour.
              Two branches perfectly balancing each other.

GRIOT   A living fossil, perhaps the oldest type of tree under
              the sky. It's called Chastity because it's so rare :
              unlikely to find a partner.

BROOMY   She's a darling. And this magnificent horse-chestnut,
              young sticky-buds bursting into leaves and candles.

GRIOT   What branches!

BROOMY   Including us all in her arms.

GRIOT   I've sat by that ilex often, that evergreen oak by the lake.

BROOMY   That's my four-branched seat when I feed the geese.

GRIOT   What's that young, neat, unbroken one?

BROOMY   That's the hard hornbeam. Like the chestnut girl, he has both male and female seeds and pollinates himself. Dapper, with clean branches. That sort will coppice well, and make a good hedge.

GRIOT   Not here, though. But which of all these is your favourite?

BROOMY   Aha! Now the one most like me is that old copper-beech leaning right over sideways; first you see as you come in the garden. All gnarled.

Enter Koinonia.

KOINONIA   Are you talking about me? Hullo, Master.

GRIOT   Hullo, Koinonia.

BROOMY   No, dearie. I was just going to tell the Master about my strawberries. I have some strawberry beds in a manor full of lunatics near here, and they were mopping and waving at the windows. I don't usually take any notice of them, but they called out. 'What are you doing?' they said. 'I'm putting manure on my strawberries' I said. 'Come in here' they said. 'They put cream on ours on Sundays.'

GRIOT   Oxford dons, unlike soldiers, don't fade away; they just lose their faculties. Are you out for a walk?

KOINONIA   I'm just off to meet my best friend, Amatrix. She's at Cambridge. We both went up at the same time, and finish this year. We're having a few days together before Finals.

GRIOT   What better way to relax? I hope you let me meet
             her.

KOINONIA   Thank you; I will. 'Bye, Broomy. Good-bye, Master.

             Exit Koinonia.

BROOMY   If I were a young man, I could fancy her.

GRIOT   She's like your maidenhair tree, very strict and
             perfect.

BROOMY   I wish they were all like her. The popinjays! Ah!
             See that goose? It was infatuated with the male
             swan, and the male and female tried to drown it,
             hold its head down. But the funny thing is, when
             the cygnets came along the swans put up with it and
             allowed it food before themselves along with their
             cygnets. Now the cygnets have gone, the goose is
             distantly tolerated, provided it swims along behind
             them. Look! It's short-sighted, sees the bread last.

GRIOT   Were those little boys fishing?

BROOMY   Ah, young rascals! Do you know, there are over two
             million people fishing in England today. The same
             old trout, bream and carp must be caught again and
             again. They're so greedy! Every time they bite the
             corned beef they get hauled out by the mouth.
             Fortunately, people are careful taking out the hook.
             Even so, just imagine! They earn their keep by
             being caught. (*Pause*) By the way, what happened
             to your father? He was taken abroad, wasn't he?
             Was it in France?

GRIOT   A trumped-up charge. A howling mob. A magistrate
             frightened of a power-ridden administration. Dying
             alone, his closest friends leaving him. One can't be
             sentimental about such a death. (*Pause*) He was a
             good man.

BROOMY   They don't make them like that now. Soon be lunch.

GRIOT   Good-bye, Broomy.

Exeunt different ways.

S C E N E   T W O

A public bar.

Enter together Gan and Thalassios.

THALASSIOS   Don't sit there! That's where the homosexuals sit!

GAN   How do you define a homosexual? Like most people here fresh from school, I still prefer the company of my own sex, men rather than women, anyway. Does that make me one?

Enter Griot.

GRIOT   Hullo Thalassios, hullo Gan! May I buy you a drink?

THALASSIOS   Well that's very . . .

GAN   Thank you very much. Have you just come back from abroad?

GRIOT   From Egypt's Thebes – where a great civilization crystallized its solutions. What'll you have?

THALASSIOS   We've been drinking whisky; is that all right?

GRIOT   Whisky it is. Three, please. What about this? It's about Lebanon, my favourite country. Just before this civil war began, the President decided that his Administration lacked something – panoply, prestige; so he called his Government together and told them

to form a committee to procure a Sputnik. Lebanon
would then be honoured as a power with a satellite
in space. This they did, but there was then a
problem. It was one thing to procure the hardware
but quite another to find an astronaut to drive the
old-fashioned manned satellite. There was only one
thing to do, so they advertised in the *New York
Herald Tribune*.

The first to be interviewed by their three-man committee was a Frenchman. 'Good!' they said,
'Welcome! And would you say how much you'd
charge?' 'Three million dollars', he replied. They
were not prepared for such an astronomic sum, but
kept their cool and asked him how he could
justify that figure. 'I will need one million dollars for
my wife, in case I never return', he said, 'one million
to keep my mistress from visiting my wife while I'm
away, and one for myself.' Put like this it sounded
more reasonable, so they asked him to write it down
as his formal proposal and wait outside.

The next was an American; fully experienced and
in top physical condition. 'Good!' said the Chairman, 'Welcome! And how much would you charge?'
'Six million', said the American. They were a little
startled. 'Oh. And how do you make up your
account?' 'One million for my wife, kids, insurance,
hire purchase payments, mortgage, possible mortuary
expenses and fund for my return. Two to provide
media-coverage for you over the whole operation.
And three to pay for my replacement in the base-
ball team.' 'Ah! Now we see', they said. 'Would you
mind putting it in writing and waiting outside?'

The last applicant was Lebanese. 'How much?' they
said. 'Nine million', he replied. 'How on earth do you
arrive at such a sum?' 'Well, gentlemen', said the
Lebanese, 'the first three million – for having the
courage and perception to choose me – is for your-

selves. (*Pause*) The second three million is for my administrative ability, managerial skills, my family, the maintenance of my business while I'm away, and to act as cushion money for my wife on discovering that I have accepted such an assignment.' (*Long pause*)

'And what', said the Chairman, 'about the remaining three million? Have you a use for that?'

'Oh!' said the Lebanese. 'Did I forget to say? That's to pay the Frenchman for doing the job.'

GAN   I went over Lebanon once by air. It made me want to try some real rock-climbing. I've read Whymper's *Scrambles amongst the Alps*, Mummery's *My Climbs in the Alps*, and Leslie Stephen's *The Playground of Europe*.

GRIOT   I hope you go, as a change from your jungle-studies. What about you, Thalassios?

THALASSIOS   I've been boating round Scotland, studying whisky.

GRIOT   Can you distinguish one from another? Is the bouquet different?

THALASSIOS   Not bouquet! The 'nose', Master, that's what the true whisky-tasters call it. You can tell a malt by the 'nose'. (*Sniffs*) There's even a 'nose-glass'.

GAN   Surely you can tell by the colour?

THALASSIOS   Whisky comes off the still like gin, colourless. Its colour comes in the cask. If it's held in a cask that's contained sweet sherry, some of the tint in the wood seeps back over the years into the whisky. Then, if the cask is used again, the tint is less, though it's still there. If you're a real professional, you will be able to tell the difference between a malt matured in an already-used sweet-sherry cask, and one that's been held in a first-time-round dry-sherry cask.

GRIOT   Can you?

THALASSIOS   Not yet. But anyway, nowadays the brewers are rogues. They add colour, and measure the artificial colouring with a tintometer.

GAN   A tintometer!

GRIOT   No-one seems to know the chemistry of distilling. People have tried using exactly the same methods in other countries, but it doesn't work.

THALASSIOS   It's a miracle, a mystique!

GRIOT   It's something to do with the humidity of the atmosphere.

THALASSIOS   It's worth the attention of an entire lifetime. And I'm afraid I'm not one of those who swill it round their mouth and spit it out. Always taste when your palate is pristine, in top condition. Before breakfast. One meal, or one cigarette, and it's ruined. If we're serious we should do all our whisky-drinking before breakfast.

GAN   Any illumination would soon be darkened! Could you tell me how I might learn to fly?

GRIOT   There's the local flying squadron.

THALASSIOS   Have you done any?

GRIOT   I had an instructor who used to make me try to land on a cloud. You'd feel the kite begin to spin like a sycamore. One's instinctive reaction is to pull back the stick. That's why many pilots die in the early stages. They don't realize that when you start the spin, and see the ground going round and round towards you, you should continue down to gather speed enough to enable you to fly out of the spin on the far side.

GAN   It's not only what you know, it's who you learned it from. That information may one day save my life.

GRIOT   But *you* know the land. You know it as well as a poacher.

GAN   Wind and the stars are the poacher's guide. It's the fog that leads him astray.

Exeunt, the two younger men unsteadily.

SCENE THREE

Enter Koinonia and Amatrix

KOINONIA   It's a day when perfection has got in the way of efficiency.

AMATRIX   I've been longing to see you. What fun! I love Cambridge, but I'm always thinking of you over here. Now I can see what you're doing.

KOINONIA   Instead of your great chapels, here we have huge dining-halls.

AMATRIX   I wish I had breasts like yours. When I woke this morning mine were all firm. I felt, 'This is it. Lovely!'

KOINONIA   I like your chestnut shoes!

AMATRIX   They'll have to last now. I'm all interested in ancestors. Do you know yours? I've just heard that, in the children's home, people wanting to adopt came to look over some of us in our prams, and they

didn't even bother to put the blanket back over *me*.
I got sunstroke. Bit of a rejection, don't you think?

KOINONIA   Demoralizing. I remember my sister in her pram, the
canopy up. We were always told to take care to keep
the sun off her.

AMATRIX   You said you remember the day she was born. You
were packed off to a Punch and Judy show and your
brother fell out of the apple-tree and broke his arm.
It's so exciting! One moment there was just you
two, and then you knew she was there and you
had a sister! I've never thought of that before. I
don't know a single person who was present – or
even knew – when I was born.

KOINONIA   Are there no photos?

AMATRIX   Nothing. Just the medical record. I don't really know
what a relative is. Most people grow up loving their
parents. It's so normal they don't even think about
it. But I can't even imagine what it's like. I won't
know till I have a baby. Is that bond different from
just loving someone because you have been brought
up by them? I don't know. It confuses me so much,
the idea of brothers and sisters being more than
friends.

KOINONIA   No pictures of your mother?

AMATRIX   Nothing from the day she turned her back for never.
Why doesn't my mother let me see her? Doesn't
she know I can see her every time I look in the
mirror?

KOINONIA   Who knows where she is! I'm sure once a year when
your birthday comes round she remembers, and
wonders.

AMATRIX   A shadow lives because I block the light. She probably dreads me. Yet I'm here, is there any doubt about that?

KOINONIA   (*Laughing*) No doubt. But I'm the other way round. I'd hate to meet clones. And as for carbon-copy humans, I hope they never succeed in making them.

AMATRIX   So do I. Friends are the most important things really.

KOINONIA   I suppose a friend is someone who doesn't mind if he or she has heard it before. A brother or sister does.

AMATRIX   Women need reassurance far more than men. We wilt and lose confidence without it. Do you think we feel the world and men owe us something? We don't want to be self-sufficient?

KOINONIA   Well I do. I'm not a real person as a student. I'm really looking forward to having a job and flat of my own, with a place in the world. In a way that will be my reassurance.

AMATRIX   (*Very serious*) The fact that a woman can have fewer genetic reproduction opportunities than a man – only one a year instead of at least three hundred and sixty-five – must make her more selective.

KOINONIA   (*Laughing*) And quicker to move on if she has not found the right mate.

AMATRIX   And more intense when she thinks she has. So of course men are more promiscuous. It would be genetically odd if they weren't. Who are they?

KOINONIA   Two friends. Come and meet them.

SCENE FOUR

Enter Gan and Thalassios.

KOINONIA   Gan, this is Amatrix; Amatrix this is Thalassios.
            She's over from Cambridge, and my best friend. Will
            you help show her around?

GAN   Yippee!

AMATRIX   Pardon?

THALASSIOS Let's all go punting!

KOINONIA   Well not immediately, thank you all the same.
            Amatrix has only just arrived off the train and needs
            to unpack.

AMATRIX   I'd love to later.

GAN   Great! Good journey?

AMATRIX   There was a girl weeping at Oxford station saying
            good-bye to her mother. She was going back to
            boarding-school. 'I miss you too!' the mother was
            saying and got on the train, and then the poor girl
            had to console her weeping mother, and push her
            off!

KOINONIA   There are shadows of sun on the grass. A warm day
            ahead, but still a cool breeze. We'll meet you here,
            later.

AMATRIX   'Bye!

Exeunt Koinonia and Amatrix.

THALASSIOS & GAN	'Bye!
GAN	Isn't she an apple?
THALASSIOS	I'd fall for Koinonia.
GAN	'Daphne with her thighs in bark.' All right! That's settled. A foursome.

SCENE FIVE

Enter Fashshar.

GAN	Here's fiery Fashshar.
THALASSIOS	Hullo, Fashshar! What do you think of those two?
FASHSHAR	Hullo dear boys.
THALASSIOS	Oh, don't lord it over us. You may be a don, but you're not much over thirty.
FASHSHAR	That's why I prefer the company of undergraduates to that of my colleagues.
GAN	Especially if the undergraduates are female.
THALASSIOS	What do you think of the two who've just left?
FASHSHAR	I've just come from destroying a colleague's reputation in a lecture, and wasn't concentrating.
GAN & THALASSIOS	(*Mocking*) No, you haven't?
FASHSHAR	(*Mock-modestly*) Well, I know one of them, the untouchable Koinonia. But who's with her?

GAN   Her budding Cambridge friend, Amatrix.

FASHSHAR   Oh yes. They say she sticks only with girls.

GAN   I hope not!

FASHSHAR   Interested? Fascinated by a gynandromorph, are you?
               Better than Koinonia, I suppose – that garden statue
               made not of stone but of concrete.

THALASSIOS   Who would be your choice, Fashshar?

FASHSHAR   My interest in the opposite sex is exponential; it
               increases in proportion to the amount available.

GAN   Doctor Fashshar, expert in iatrogenia.

THALASSIOS   What's that?

GAN   Disease caused by the doctor's face, treatment and
               suggestions.

FASHSHAR   My kingdom is not of medicine.

THALASSIOS   What do you advise, Fashshar, as an older and more
               experienced man?

GAN   So we can listen and do the opposite.

FASHSHAR   If you want Koinonia, suck an icicle. Gan, are you
               after that new bird?

GAN   I should like to be her escort for her visit.

FASHSHAR   If you want more than that you'd better try a crafty
               device, a cautel, a stratagem : dress as a woman.

GAN   She's a gem and I need no strategy.

THALASSIOS   Why not try it, Gan? See if she'd notice. What a laugh!

GAN   Say the Master met me with her! I'd feel such an ape.

THALASSIOS   Oh, he understands men; he's a born leader.

GAN   In a way, yes. But he tends to value people on their own estimate of themselves.

FASHSHAR   That's not a bad criterion in the first instance.

GAN   But say he saw me as a woman? All right. Just for the hell of it.

FASHSHAR   Gentlemen, Mara is approaching, we are coming in to land. Please will you return to your sexes? We hope you have enjoyed your earache. Please make sure your seatbelts are insecure. The mortuary is sorry for the inconvenience caused by the redevelopment of terminal facilities.

SCENE   SIX

Enter Mara.

MARA   Are you scouting for talent?

FASHSHAR   Are you scouting for boys? I feel like a derelict suitcase left when the coach has departed.

MARA   Yes, you should be kept locked up. What are you telling these . . . men?

FASHSHAR   That living as we are at the end of time, our obsession with sex is like a dying man's erection, a final fierce reassertion of Nature against the inevitable.

THALASSIOS   He was giving advice on how we should approach the two girls who were here.

MARA   Was one Koinonia? She'll make you put on your suit to watch the Queen on telly.

THALASSIOS   That's most unfair!

MARA   Unfortunately for her, one day she'll fall in love with the man she's going out with.

GAN   And what's wrong with that?

MARA   It's putting the donkey before the dowry.

FASHSHAR   Both sinister and gauche. Money talks; it says 'Goodbye'. You said you had the lecture-hall key, Gan. May I have it, so we can close the building?

GAN   It's in my room.

FASHSHAR   Thalassios, I leave you to the pleasure of a magnificent woman.

Exeunt Fashshar and Gan.

SCENE SEVEN

THALASSIOS   So you know each other well?

MARA   We haven't been going out together very long. I'm not married any more, and I've only seen him regularly since all that was over. It's such a relief being single again. If I'm out with a man, I don't have to rush back and clean up and think of an alibi.

THALASSIOS   I should have thought too much adultery would wear out any marriage.

MARA   It's not the act of adultery that ages you so much as all the things that go with it – getting up in a hurry, putting mascara in your eye before you've recovered, slinking in at the right time, car journeys. One of my ovaries has been removed.

THALASSIOS   Which can't you have, a boy or a girl?

MARA   (*Laughing*) Silly boy! What's your secret love?

THALASSIOS   The sea. Isn't it your life? I wish it were mine.

MARA   Come and try!

THALASSIOS   Are you in the Royal Navy?

MARA   The most women get on in the Royal Navy is a canal boat. They never go to sea. I'm in the Merchant Navy.

THALASSIOS   Do you like it?

MARA   I love the sea. I'm married to it. But I'm careful. You have to take care of your name at sea. Everything follows you: when shoreside again, on the next boat, when you're applying for another job.

THALASSIOS   But surely you've firm friends who'll stick up for you?

MARA   They are married, don't want to see you on shore when they're with their boy-friends or husbands, in case you say something about what they've been doing at sea. You can understand it.

THALASSIOS   Why is there so much gossip?

MARA   Well, on nearly every ship there is a communal seat in the main alleyway. If a girl has spent the night anywhere other than her own accommodation she

is bound to be spotted as all the cabins lead off the
main alleyway. By the time she goes down to work,
everyone that's passed the 'park bench' has heard
where she's been, and of anyone else that had been
seen going back to her cabin as well. For about a
day she's ridiculed and the story's distorted, and
then it's forgotten; unless she makes a habit of sleeping out.

THALASSIOS   What's the average age of these gossip-mongers?

MARA   About thirty-five . . . to fifty. There's not really a lot
else to talk about. I must admit to being guilty of
this myself. You live, breathe and eat these other
people you work with for at least six weeks, and
there are a lot of people at sea whose lives revolve
around other people's problems.

THALASSIOS   Do you fall for the men?

MARA   Oh, I used to at first, but I learned. They all have
wives or boy-friends at home. Really proves the point
about all at sea being a false existence, doesn't it?
Or homosexual. I go out when I'm ashore. No-one
knows what you do then. If you sleep with fifty men
at home, you can only go out with one on a ship,
otherwise you're a slag. Then you spoil your chances
for the future.

THALASSIOS   That's why you're going out with Fashshar?

MARA   A bit stormy. I'm not sure I like it. But I feel a kind
of knickerless content when I've been with him.

THALASSIOS   I'm fascinated. How do you live on the ship?

MARA   Usually four girls to a cabin. After you've done a
couple of trips on a ship you usually choose the girls
you share with – and even then things can go wrong.
If one of the girls is 'boxed off' as we call it, and she

brings her man to the cabin, you can hear them going all night. A bit off-putting. The other girls never ask if you mind! You've only got a curtain and a bunk-light. One evening I got really angry and swore at them to stop and get out, and the whispers stopped and there was a lot of fumbling, and they left. Nothing was ever said afterwards.

THALASSIOS   Could put thoughts in your head.

MARA   You find the boy-friend creeps in at two a.m., and no way can you get back to sleep for about an hour. One time I was in the top bunk sharing with three other girls, and the girl beneath me claimed to be a virgin! First virgin I ever knew had so many men through her bed. Besides her, the other girls used to entertain most evenings as well.

THALASSIOS   Doesn't anyone ever object?

MARA   Well, there's the female crew's stewardess. We call her the Glory-Hole, as she's in charge of the lavatories. She acts a bit like a warden. She doesn't mind if you're going steady, but a good one draws the line at anything else. It gets the cabin a bad name.

THALASSIOS   I was going to meet Koinonia here. Don't talk sex to her, will you?

MARA   She's no one to point the finger, poor frustrated girl. Don't the real men prefer the challenge of a woman with personality, instead of a little wife who only wants peace, no tantrums, calm, order, no demands?

Enter Fashshar with lewd magazine.

MARA   Where have you been with that magazine? Come on, sing!

FASHSHAR   Peeling French belles. Hullo, ship's timber! Green as ever? What have you been doing with Mara?

THALASSIOS   I'm waiting for Koinonia, but she must be looking for me somewhere else.

MARA   She called me tulips.

THALASSIOS   Why?

MARA   Because she said my two lips were always gossiping.

FASHSHAR   There are only two sorts of women; those that do and those that don't. And I don't want to waste time with the don'ts. Come on, Mara – shall we investigate?

MARA   Invaginate, you mean.

Exeunt Fashshar and Mara one way, Thalassios the other.

SCENE EIGHT

Enter Griot, Koinonia and Amatrix

GRIOT   And so they come, jewellers and speculators on earnest feet.

AMATRIX   But don't you feel, living in College all the year round, like being in a perpetual sauna-bath? Hot term, cold vacation, hot term again?

KOINONIA   These violent swings from one background to another – totally opposite – one, make it very difficult for me to settle at home.

GRIOT   Do you mean all the time you wish you were back here?

AMATRIX   They say 'You waste your time reading when you could be working!'

KOINONIA   When I go home I never know how to tell them when I'm going back. If I say at the beginning of the holiday, they think I'm counting the days before I can be back in my College room again. If I tell them half-way through, they think I'm beginning to grow bored; and if I leave it until nearly the last moment and say I'm panicking about my work, they say I'm springing it on them, and they'd arranged all sorts of visits to relations during the last few days before term. Yet I can't read a book at home. I have to come back a few days early. Every day there's something perfectly legitimate. 'You haven't seen your aunt for eighteen months. You must come downstairs and say 'Hello!'' Then the afternoon's shot!

GRIOT   Perhaps your parents could be trained to ask how long you can stay for when you first go home. That would take the burden off you, and let them know well in advance. They could gradually become accustomed to it. They might even be able to plan their own lives.

AMATRIX   Don't you find they can't ask, because it would mean accepting the fact that you don't live there any more, you only visit? And the neat room they've been keeping for you isn't really going to see much of you in future?

GRIOT   The longer you live with memories, the fresher they become. That's why the past seems so near.

AMATRIX   (*Indignant*) And why won't parents act on what we tell them? Especially those living abroad under impossible regimes.

GRIOT   After a certain age you do not leave property, home

and roots and settle with nothing in a new environ-
ment, however great the political pressure. 'Better to
die soon where you are than slowly elsewhere in
despair.'

KOINONIA   Do you believe that?

GRIOT   I do not.

AMATRIX   I know what you mean. Those attitudes caused the
two World Wars.

GRIOT   The values of courtesy and honour are good. In the
First World War they were misused, and now they're
under attack. But that doesn't make them wrong.

KOINONIA   Can't the press play an important part? Can't they
expose the torture-doctors?

GRIOT   What do you think? The press is interested in what
is urgent, not in what is important. Why does no
Sunday Paper carry a column analysing contem-
porary sermons? Yet the Oxford Professors review
rubbish weekly for their own self-aggrandizement.
Some of the finest brains in the country are exercised
publicly in cathedrals every week on the most search-
ing topics; and the press pays not a second's attention.

KOINONIA   It's hard, growing up.

AMATRIX   It's important, if you feel happy, to tell people you
are. If you like a girl's dress, to go up and tell her
so! Not many people do. But I'm always glad when
I've done it!

GRIOT   (*Amused*) You'll have a wonderful life ahead of you.

KOINONIA   (*To Amatrix*) I'm not sure I wouldn't be a little
suspicious. Oh, not with you – but then I know
you! Master; you always seem just a little sad. Are
you?

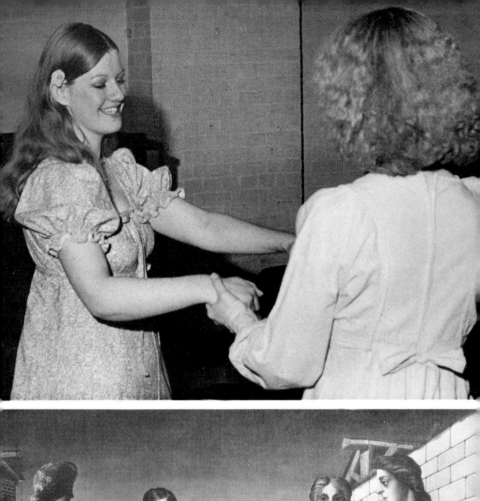

GRIOT   Koinonia, no.

AMATRIX   Perhaps people expect a Master to be grave.

GRIOT   The weakness of democracy is that it puts its faith
            in the mystique of status, not in the qualities of the
            man.

KOINONIA   Are you happy?

GRIOT   One can be intoxicated by beauty in all its forms –
            human, divine, food, flowers, music, young people in
            love – and yet be aware . . .

KOINONIA   Aware of what?

GRIOT   Koinonia, aware that the hammer and sickle is the
            cross and crescent combined. Amatrix, you know
            those angels high on the organ of King's?

AMATRIX   One with a trumpet?

GRIOT   Do you think Shakespeare just couldn't resist making
            that his emblem of pity when he stood there? 'Plead
            like angels trumpet-tongued . . .'? Strange.

AMATRIX   How odd a trumpet-blast should be a plea!

GRIOT   I have kept you too long.

KOINONIA   I've longed to keep you a little; if only to ask my
            question, and to let you see my friend.

GRIOT   Amatrix, see me again. Koinonia, you're always
            welcome.

            Koinonia and Amatrix exeunt.

Enter Fashshar.

FASHSHAR   Ah Griot!

GRIOT   Hullo Fashshar! How is your new pupil surviving
with you?

FASHSHAR   Mara? We had one of the best week-ends ever. On
Friday evening she suddenly said that she 'felt it
was not right to be going out with an older man'.
Me! From what she had heard from her friends,
these things never worked out. I could probably
adjust easily to a break-up, whereas if she got any
more involved she would find it very difficult to start
again. (*Pause*) Then we had the best week-end ever.
Sex good, the sun shone, everything. Then Sunday
lunchtime she brought it up again. I said 'Have
some self-confidence Mara! I don't want a woman-
friend who's not going to grow up and let me help
her to grow.' She kept saying that she felt over-.
shadowed by me. Griot: I want a girl who is proud
of me, of what I'm doing; who shares what she is
doing and asks me, 'Am I being silly?' She just
clammed up in company, was jealous of my women
friends, and afraid when my male colleagues came
round. Sullen. Obstinate.

GRIOT   She seems entirely different to me.

FASHSHAR   Well anyway. We had agreed to go to Greece together in August. Only a few nights before, as we
were walking around Oxford, she'd said, 'I'd love to
be cooking some Greek food for you on the beach
now!' 'Ah, ha!' I thought. 'This is what it's all
about. We may be going through a dull patch, but
it's worth it if it's leading up to something – the
holiday in Greece together. She's been there before

and I haven't. She can teach me for a change, and restore her self-confidence.' (*Pause*) Then suddenly she says on this Sunday afternoon, 'I'm having a month in Greece on my own this August.' Well! I tell you frankly, I went off in a huff. I walked in the sunshine and saw all those beautiful girls in the streets asking me to parties and on the river, and I made up my mind then. If she apologizes and says it was all a mistake and we plan the holiday, I'll go on with the relationship; but if not. . . .

Well, do you know what she said when I walked back after this decision? 'Have you recovered?' 'Whether or not I've recovered,' I said, 'this is the end of our association.' She didn't speak a word from that moment on. I called a taxi, gave her some money for it, helped her in to it. I meant it. I passed her a day or two later on my bicycle and I waved and smiled, and she blushed on the pavement and looked sheepish. But I didn't stop. No ill feelings. I'd done the decent thing.

GRIOT   And now you're back together.

FASHSHAR   (*Abashed*) Eh? Oh. (*Pause*)

GRIOT   I know she was hurt.

FASHSHAR   My dear Master, so was I! If I'm denied advancement due to my abilities I will of course become jaundiced and violent.

GRIOT   Couldn't intelligence join hands with affection?

FASHSHAR   She was completely outcountenanced.

GRIOT   The pub was shut, so they put her in the garage.

FASHSHAR   Why do you mock me?

GRIOT   No mocking. Come and see my new Paul Delvaux
               lithograph over a drink.

               Exeunt.

               SCENE TEN

               Broomy. Enter to him Gan, dressed as a girl.

BROOMY   (*Working*) Mornin', ma'am.

GAN   Good, Broomy. You restore my lack of faith in myself.

BROOMY   Oh, you students! Books have made you barmy.
               What are you doing in that get-up?

GAN   I'm infatuated with the most beautiful girl, Broomy.
               You've seen her.

BROOMY   One of them two young misses?

GAN   Yes. The golden one. Over from Cambridge.

BROOMY   Do you think you'll fool her!

GAN   I did you, Broomy!

BROOMY   Naah! I knew all the time.

GAN   Do you think it will work?

BROOMY   What? She'll fall for you dressed like a clown?

GAN   I'm not dressed like a clown!

BROOMY   Listen to me, Mr Gan. Some things you must never
               do; some things you must always do. Never have
               lilac in the house. No peacock's feathers. Mustn't
               cross knives at the table. If you spill salt, you must
               throw a pinch over your left shoulder to keep the

devil away. Never put the tea in first, or you'll have red-headed children; and a man should never dress as a woman.

GAN   Oh, Broomy! Every pantomime has one. Or more!

BROOMY   I can't help your high culture. Just an excuse for a lot of dirt, if you ask me. You'd do better to look in the church where your names is carved.

GAN   I hope mine isn't.

BROOMY   'Never shed a tear', said my old wife, God bless her, 'till you can't roll a bowl.' When I can't put a wood up the green (*Bowling gesture*) it's time to leave this world.

GAN   Have you seen any other students come this way?

BROOMY   Undergraduates? They all come up with holes in their shoes. Mad dress. Loud laughs and trample on my flowerbeds. Now look at these fritillaries. Beautiful! White, or snake-speckled purple flower-bell hanging down. Look at this white one! Six green streaks along the vein of the bell, and six green stamens inside.

GAN   Have you ever seen a fox in this garden?

BROOMY   All sorts. Policeman, he says to me he's seen him in Carfax at four in the morning. In from Radley. Knows when it's dustbin day. You can hear him. His warble is like the sound of a circular saw biting on bone. If it rains on apple-christening day, it's going to rain for forty days. I wish they'd fit loud-speakers in that library. Then I could hear when the librarian's going to lunch. Can't abide him. I always seem to be going through the gate at the same time. Yours is a nice girl. She doesn't want her man in bonnet and handbag!

GAN   It's a stratagem. Here she comes!

            Enter Amatrix

BROOMY   She's not like that older one who don't go back to
             her lodgings till the birds sing in the morning. Hullo,
             Miss!

AMATRIX   Hullo, Broomy! How old are you?

BROOMY   Young as my old body can expect.

AMATRIX   I'm as well as my mind will allow me. Hullo. Broomy,
             will you introduce me?

BROOMY   No I won't, Miss, but I wish you well. (*Exit*)

GAN   (*High voice*) I'm looking for Gan.

AMATRIX   Are you his sister? We were going to meet here.

GAN   Yes. Isn't he nice?

AMATRIX   He is. I've only just met him. People are so friendly
             here. You're like a girl I had a pash on at school.

GAN   They weren't allowed at mine.

AMATRIX   Did you have them all the same? We used to leave
             notes in a collecting-box at Christmas. It was awful
             if you didn't receive any.

GAN   When I was very small, I left my dinner-money on
             my friend's ink-well. It just fitted the empty hole.
             She took it up to the teacher, and the teacher stood
             in front of the whole class and asked, 'Who has left
             their coin on Pauline's desk?' I was so embarrassed.
             I said 'Me', but couldn't explain why. Pauline never
             knew anything of my feelings.

AMATRIX   We used to try to find little jobs to do for ours. I made a tiny hexagonal box to hold a tooth of hers, and covered it in blue patterned cotton so that one tiny flower filled each of the panels. It was so small, I couldn't do it now my fingers have grown.

GAN   In some ways I wish we could keep that innocence.

AMATRIX   What's wrong with your voice?

GAN   (*Stifled laugh*) Nothing. (*Sneezes*)

AMATRIX   (*Seeing through disguise*) Haven't we met before?

GAN   (*Normal voice*) You win. I wondered how long I could keep it up.

AMATRIX   (*Laughing*) You madman! How can you punt in that?

GAN   I had hoped Thalassios would do the work. Will you come to an old lady's party on Thursday?

AMATRIX   What old lady?

GAN   You'll need to know the background. Back in the twenties this old lady had been to a house-party exactly like the one she's giving next week. A man in a velvet jacket had chatted her up, and later in the evening, during a game of 'Murder', she had gone into a dark place with him. They were silent, except for the fact that at one point in a melancholy tone he had recited a poem to her, an obvious invitation to make love, after which, still in silence, they did. The poem was something like this:

> May you live as long as you want.
> May you want to as long as you live.
> If I'm asleep and you want me, wake me.
> If I'm awake and don't want to, make me.

> Kings and Queens do it and sigh,
> Little bees do it – buzz buzz – and die.
> But *I* can't do it, and I'll tell you why :
> Because I have a lover, and I've promised to
>   be true.
> But I'll tell you what I'll do –
> I'll lie still and let you.

When she reached for the light afterwards and switched it on, she found it was not her flatterer in the velvet coat at all but her brother, who had deliberately swapped jackets in the game. They never talked of it again. He went into the RAF, became a pilot, was shot down at the Battle of Britain and killed. Now in her old age she is haunted by the incident, and in order to exorcize the memory – and perhaps to understand her brother better, who she is certain could never have written the poem – she's obsessed with finding out where the poem came from. Do you know? It might throw light on what her brother was reading, a song he was singing, a French poem he might have been translating, at the time. Hence this second house-party. Can you come?

AMATRIX   How odd! No, I'll have left by then. I'll never forget that story. 'May you live as long as you want . . .' Why don't you go and change, and come with us?

GAN   I'll be delighted. Come! Let's go.

Exeunt.

SCENE ELEVEN

Enter Koinonia and Thalassios.

KOINONIA   They're not here!

THALASSIOS   Then there's Tom of the Funeral Parlour. They say he does Bed and Breakfast for one pound fifty above the parlour. I told him when I came to him I wouldn't be needing breakfast.

KOINONIA   I used to love listening to the soothing ghost in the grandfather-clock. I would *always* return to my father to help him if he needed me; wouldn't you?

THALASSIOS   If I could. But I'm a wanderer. I'd feel jailed; becalmed.

KOINONIA   And there was this horrid book called *Shock-Headed Peter* with a scissor-man who came when the boy was alone, and chopped off his thumbs for sucking them.

Enter Mara.

MARA   Koinonia, do you ever have the feeling, on Saturday nights, that you are being chaste?

KOINONIA   Mara, you have such a sharp tongue that I'd rather have you as an enemy than a friend.

MARA   Oh, come.

KOINONIA   If I were on your boat I'd jump over the side.

MARA   If you say anything about jumping over they lock you up at once. They always seem to leave their shoes behind! You wear the same shoes all the time at sea, and you're walking in the galley all the time, so your shoes get ruined. You come to recognize people by their shoes, know them without looking up.

THALASSIOS   I know mine are ruined after a week-end's sailing.

MARA   (*Paying full attention to Thalassios*) I was working in the laundry aft of the ship. It's always at 4.15. The ship slows down. There're usually three or four officers at the gunport door, and they lower the canvas after a few prayers over the side.

THALASSIOS   Don't they hold on till the next port?

MARA   Not now. They don't keep corpses in fridges any more at sea. Soon as anyone dies, plop! over the side. The canvas was so thick it bounced five or six times. The ship was moving so fast it wouldn't go down for ages. Imagine the wash on a thirty-six-thousand-ton liner!

THALASSIOS   Don't they mind?

MARA   Who? The passengers? Oh, some ships are happy ships. You walk on a ship and you know at once instinctively whether you'll be happy or not. If you're not liked it can be hell. It's no use complaining when you reach land. No one will talk. One boy was unpopular and taken outside his cabin, and now can't see through his left eye. He had to continue working the rest of the trip. A big padded bandage over his eye.

KOINONIA   How vile!

Enter Amatrix.

AMATRIX   There you are!

MARA   (*To Amatrix*) Let's go and stand on the flyover with bright knickers on and watch the cars swerve as they look up!

AMATRIX   (*Laughing*) Light skirts and no pants!

THALASSIOS   (*Laughs inordinately*).

MARA   (*To Thalassios*) You like the idea? Come and watch, then!

KOINONIA   You'd justify taking anyone's husband.

AMATRIX   (*Friendly*) A single girl of your age and looks is a threat to married women!

MARA   Well, I've got to have my sex, just as any wife must. Most of the men I take are not having it with their wives anyway, and the wives are at fault for that; so why not please them and myself at the same time? Who knows? What's lost?

KOINONIA   Call in the friendly neighbourhood spiv, will you?

MARA   (*To amuse Amatrix and Thalassios, and to shock Koinonia*) I've a thirty-five-year-old friend, two 'A'-levels, who's on the game for some money to buy a house, and her boy-friend's a mini-cab driver. Oh, you in Oxford are totally out of touch! London's where it's at. Anyway, she 'phones him when she 'goes case', tells him which hotel she's going to, and he waits outside in his mini-cab to drive her home. The only thing that makes him mad is if she takes off her wig when she's with a punter.

KOINONIA   Look; I've had enough.

AMATRIX   (*Gently*) Let her finish.

MARA   (*Enjoying the effect*) She found out he was having an affair with a young girl who lived across the road. Their home's in Kent. When he was away one night, she went across and took her out – she was young and naïve – and got her drunk at a pub, then asked her back, and got her more drunk in her flat, then gave her a kiss and told her to come on. She got her really randy, and they were just going to make it when she went into the kitchen and came back with the rolling-pin and made love to her with that. Then she said, 'Make it with my old man once more, and I'll tell him what you've done tonight!' She's thirty-five, looking far older. Been at it ten years too long. (*To Thalassios*) Are you coming?

THALASSIOS   (*To Koinonia*) You don't mind, do you?

KOINONIA   No.

Mara and Thalassios exeunt.

SCENE TWELVE

KOINONIA   (*Furious*) Oooooh!

AMATRIX   She is funny! But she's stolen your man! What about our foursome?

KOINONIA   Let him go. It was proving pretty hard work, anyway. Listen! There's the perfect fifth that Carfax makes with Tom.

AMATRIX   Mine turned up in woman's clothes and took me in for a few minutes. He's a strange one. Told me an odd story that put me off him a bit.

KOINONIA   I like him.

AMATRIX   And I rather fancy Thalassios.

KOINONIA   Even though he's being initiated by Mara? (*Pause*) How weak of him!

AMATRIX   I don't mind. Do you have a boy-friend?

KOINONIA   We could swap. Eh? Oh, not really. I tried. After five weeks I could see he wasn't happy in my company, but he couldn't bring himself to say it, so one night after a film he drove me home and I said, 'Why don't you admit you don't really want to be tied down?' I had to do it for him – for his sake, and for my own self-respect. Then I cried, and he comforted me; and I said 'You aren't *supposed* to be doing this.' He only put his arm round me. Never saw him again. What about you at the moment?

AMATRIX   The man I really liked is called Straw. The sort of man who embodies the King's style; you know, tenor choral scholar who refers to Chapel as 'the God-box' and can be heard warming up singing the top notes of *This is the Record of John* in the basement of Gibbs before Evensong. (*Sings*) '. . . from Jerusalem, from Jerusalem'. (*Pause*) I used to go just to look at him in the candlelight.

KOINONIA   (*Laughing*) Does he know?

AMATRIX   Oh, I doubt it. He's beyond the sea somewhere, so at last I'm settling down to some work.

KOINONIA   (*Laughing*) How does your tutor put up with you?

AMATRIX   I had been lying in a punt all morning counting the copper-beeches along the river, forgetting the time, and had to skip lunch, as I'd a Supervision at three, and had been told to attend in Clare Garden as it was too hot to be inside. I hurried past the lavender, under that imitation fan-vault by the Porter's Lodge, but on my way to the bridge caught sight of two newly-painted golden pineapples on the roof high against the sky. Why on earth was the one above the Dining Hall folded up, while the one above the Chapel was spread out ready for eating? That really made me hungry, and I hoped my tummy wouldn't rumble while I was reading my essay. I could always cough, if it didn't happen too often; but then he would go and fetch me a glass of water – he's that

type. There he was, waiting. I sat in the garden
surrounded by neat yew-hedges staring into the pool
wishing it were tea-time, while my Supervisor droned
on about Sir Walter Raleigh and the School of
Night in the sunshine. A butterfly settled on my
hand and opened its wings and closed them with a
little tremble before fluttering off behind me. I
thought I could hear Straw's voice on the river, but
the evergreens muffled the river-sounds and I
couldn't be sure. Who's he out with? I wondered
whether the ilex would outlast the hornbeam. If it
is him on the punt, has he noticed the flying man
with a harp and the dolphin-horse carved on the
bridge? (*Pause*) 'Are you feeling well?' What could
I say? I'd forgotten all about *Love's Labour's Lost*.
I just burst into tears, yet I was happy. (*Pause*) He
didn't know what to do. It had never happened to
him before. I made an excuse and left, and bumped
straight into Straw and in full view of my Supervisor
gave a whoop of joy! You can see why he can't
make me out!

KOINONIA   You funny thing.

AMATRIX   Do you remember last year, when you came over
to Cambridge after your exams, and went back for
May Week? What did you do after you left me?

KOINONIA   After another evening spent socializing my friend
Ianthe and I escaped, pretended to go to bed. We
dressed in white, with white roses in our hair, and
slipped out the side gate to go up the Iffley Road.
Several people accosted us. We said, 'This is the
price we pay.' (It was a Perilous Quest, you see.)
We came to the gate into Christ Church meadows,
but it was locked, so we came back again and tried
another. This was shut, with spikes, but Ianthe hop-
ped over like a rabbit. Down through the meadows
by the river through a gap in the hedge. We tore
our shawls and scratched ourselves on the brambles

and barbed wire, giggling a lot. It wasn't really dark;
one in the morning on Midsummer Night. Grey,
but lifting. The trees were very big.

There was a large white ferry, the sort you pull
yourself across on with a string; but it was pad-
locked. We climbed on to it – it rocked a bit – and
went right up to the far end. All the time there was
a flute playing somewhere in a college room. We
took out the rough paper we had used in the exam
room, burnt it, and pledged we would not be caught
by the exam spirit. It flared up, and we scattered the
ashes into the dark over the water.

Then we had the half-bottle of really sour red wine
I'd bought for 40p. When I'd told the man in the
shop I was going to celebrate, he said, 'Don't go mad
with that half-bottle, will you!' Little did he know.
We drank to the Scholar Gipsy, as he'd managed
what we were trying to do; called up all the spirits
of Midsummer we could remember by name –
Queen Mab, Titania . . . poured some of the wine
into the river as a libation to the river-god.

We had a cake, and we broke it and ate a piece
each and threw some crumbly bits into the river.
Lit joss sticks; the thin smoke curled up all grey.
They stayed red for ages, little pinpoints of incense.
In the distance we could hear bells from all the
Oxford clocks, and the sounds from the Corpus Ball.
Rustling of little animals moving in the bank.

At one point I said, 'I wonder where the Spirit of
Queen Mab is?' and there was a terrific explosion –
from one of the balls, I suppose. We took the roses
out of our hair, the symbols of our fading beauty –
we are both getting on, twenty now – cupped them
in our hands and gently put them on the water.
They stayed on the surface going round and round
for a long while. I had a bicycle-lamp with me and

shone a beam of light down on them, and we
watched them for ages.

Ianthe has this lovely Hebridean accent, and sang
I once loved a lass, and I sang a French ballad about
Louis XIVth, and that's very sad too. Then the
Unquiet Grave. Then we both sang *The Skye Boat
Song* humming when we got stuck after 'Loud the
winds roar . . .'. Then we sang our talisman song *The
North Country Maid,* which we'd sung some days
going up the steps to the exams, ending, 'I wish I
were home in my own countree.'

Then it was nearly two o'clock. We had talked a
long while and were getting cold. We had to crawl
through the hedge with a front wriggle and drop
down the other side, like diving. The hems of our
dresses were damp. Ianthe had a late key. She let
me in, and nobody ever knew.

Bell for Hall rings.

AMATRIX   We must go. (*Impetuously*) I've always wanted a
sister; promise we'll be sisters always?

KOINONIA   (*Putting the palms of her hands against the palms
of Amatrix's hands*)

What is it in your walk, your face, your eyes,
So startles, lingering in the memory?
The way you talk, your grace, immortalize
These passing moments with their melody.
Time spent with you is heightened, clearer-etched
Like Evesham valley sunlit after rain,
And no ambition for you seems far-fetched
When we have met, and know we shall again.
Your voice hangs in the air, though notes have
        passed,
Like pollen filling summer nights with scent

That stirs the heart and wakes the unsurpassed
Joy that your gentle company has lent.
With you love, beauty, memory distil
A pearl of rarest truth time cannot kill.

AMATRIX   Let me confess that in my secret mind
The claw of bitterness has gripped a hold
On sad occasion, and quite undermined
The quiet hope that kept me from the cold.
Let me confess, too, that I have no cause
For cavilling, and should throw care away.
Hasn't the sun brought laughter out of doors
And spread a primrose carpet for the May?
Haven't I to my touch new leaves in bud
And music everywhere in bush and tree?
Doesn't the very air breathe likelihood
Of love united, flown across the sea?
Let me confess I have no cause for weeping;
And ask, for absolution, your safe-keeping.

Exeunt.

END OF ACT ONE

Act Two

SCENE ONE

GRIOT A fallen tree – its roots can form my backrest –
slants morning shadows in this spring wood. Birdsong
all around. Lark . . . blackbird . . . thrush . . . bull-
finch and willow-piper. Stillness caresses their song.
Now, early on Monday morning, after the first good
night's sleep for ages, I am alert in every sense. The
water swirls on, rippling and towing. Last week the
two girls were here, so full of life they embodied the
season. Now only rabbits, twigs, warm sunshine
fingering the leaves. Feel of the bark. The dignity
and formality of each tree, so different; even when
distorted, so self-assured. Endlessly changing light
through the branches on the water, in the hollows
and humps and trunks and undergrowth. Music of
peace. Sticky buds. A lungful of spiritual air with
its oxygen of quiet.

SCENE TWO

Enter Mara dressed as a man.

MARA Ah, Griot, I thought you'd be here. What I'd really
like is to find a clever and good-looking, healthy
man I could lead into marrying me – for preference,
a little bit younger – breed a healthy couple of bright

children off him, then cold-shoulder him into divorce so that he could supply me with a couple of thousand a year in alimony and a free house to live in. If you've got the children, they're always soft enough, these male judges, to hand the house over to you. Then I could brainwash the kids against their father – find fault every time he visits, writes, tries to build up a relationship with them – till he gave up; and by my middle thirties, I'd have it all!

GRIOT   Making happiness the goal instead of a by-product of living is like hunting for cream without milking the cow.

MARA   You'll help me. You know all the young men.

GRIOT   We define ourselves by what we decline.

MARA   You have an iron gentleness.

GRIOT   What about Fashshar? One of the young executives who are now dons; bustling, inflated, leisureless and proud.

MARA   You know I've tried him and want to part; but think what the break-up of an affair means from a woman's point of view! The visit to the psychiatrist, the fees. Withdrawal symptoms. Seeing only the worst in the recent past to gain balance in the present. Longing to return to the old way of love, even if it was destructive and led to this. The growing hatred of oneself, and fear that all future possible relationships will be affected. I couldn't love anyone who didn't love me wholly; and this puts new potential boy-friends off. They call it 'man-eating'.

GRIOT   Do you want me to tell you what I think?

MARA   Give me facts, not opinions.

GRIOT   Thoughts and opinions are facts, just as much as data. In fact, democracy is built on them in the form of votes.

MARA   What turns impetuous girls like me into sardonic, scheming women?

GRIOT   You sew with a red-hot needle and burnt thread.

MARA   Pah! Would you rather I were like Koinonia and Amatrix?

GRIOT   They are girls with strong boarding-school ties, trying to adapt to the heterosexual world of Oxbridge. There's a real feeling of failure if they do not get their man during their three years . . .

MARA   And a real feeling of relief for the young men if they escape their three years unscathed.

GRIOT   Yet there's a world outside. You don't have to settle by twenty-one.

MARA   I'm twenty-five.

GRIOT   Here comes your beau. Forgive me if I leave. There are complaints against him which I must study before he and I meet.

MARA   Trial by personality.

Exit Griot one way, enter Fashshar another.

SCENE THREE

FASHSHAR   Why did he leave?

MARA   A woman's valour is indiscretion.

FASHSHAR   What's happened to your sulky pouting breasts?

MARA   I'm unisex now. You men are so rôle-conscious! Like my stepfather and mother. With them, even now, I feel constricted. They always seem ready to be disapproving. It's a sign they can't cope very well with life. They need the security of 'ought' and 'ought not'. They care what you wear.

FASHSHAR   I'm going to hold you up. (*Cupping her breasts*)

MARA   (*Rejecting him*) You've always been a great support.

FASHSHAR   Withering cynicism.

MARA   Perhaps rows are creative, bringing us closer together?

FASHSHAR   They spring from the depth of the emotion.

MARA   The quality.

FASHSHAR   The tolerance of each other.

MARA   Each wants to put the other first?

FASHSHAR   And failing.

MARA   Speak for yourself.

FASHSHAR   I always do. Give it a chance. Love is the mechanism for the perpetuation of the species.

MARA   You mean sex is. I stamped on John's foot when he mentioned you in front of my husband. It was one of those moments when you realize you've stamped on the wrong foot.

FASHSHAR   You mean your ex-husband.

MARA   You don't know it all. Yes, I've been married twice. First time at sixteen. It was the only thing that could have sobered me up. I went downstairs one morning with my brother – he was five and I was seven – and there laid out on the grand piano were new clothes for both of us. 'Put them on' said my parents, 'and take one toy each and get in the car.' They drove us off to the same boarding school and left. I'll never forget that day. My brother left after three years to go to a posh school, but I stopped till I was thrown out. Then remand home after remand home. I managed to give them the slip when I was fifteen, and live on my own in Battersea. It was my own fault, really, I was caught. I applied for a job, and gave the name of a referee and he shopped me. But after that they treated me as a grown-up. They saw I knew how to survive.

FASHSHAR   Why did you marry at sixteen?

MARA   Because I was pregnant, like most girls.

FASHSHAR   Did you have an abortion?

MARA   No, Mother's a strict Catholic. I had it adopted, and he left me after ten months.

FASHSHAR   Adopted!

MARA   They gave me three days to decide whether I wanted it or not. Those were the worst days of my life. I kept thinking of him in a pram and all that. I had to decide; but I didn't want it to end up like me.

FASHSHAR   And the second husband?

MARA   I was only married three months, and as you know we broke up three months ago. He was too good at spending my money. I got tired of it.

FASHSHAR   What was he?

MARA   Ship's Purser.

FASHSHAR   Divorce?

MARA   I want a settlement – half of what he has. If he doesn't agree I'll ruin his career. I know how to. I really did like him. The first marriage was nothing, but those three months had some really good times. (*Pause*) I like married men. Let's have a world in which wives are abolished. All in common.

FASHSHAR   And at thirty-seven pensioned off.

MARA   Green-shield stamps given with intercourse, and cow-milking machines installed for the army.

FASHSHAR   Man deified by his errors.

MARA   Number Two came back from twelve weeks in Hong Kong more conventionally masculine. He'd done all the things a young man on his own in the colonies is supposed to do. I bear him no grudge for that. I'd become more feminine.

FASHSHAR   (*Startled*) Have you? In reaction to his change?

MARA   Yes, perhaps. When we first met, the difference between the sexes was less marked. Perhaps it always is at that age.

FASHSHAR   That's why student-age is the best. All is potential, only half-defined.

MARA   All those possibilities that dance on the edge of decision.

FASHSHAR   My Father was very good to my Mother. Devoted to her. Oh, he may have had casual affairs, but he kept them to himself, and after all, he was the bread-winner.

MARA   You've never talked of the sea.

FASHSHAR   Not my territory. I did go on a fourteen-day trip to Casablanca once. We went into Las Palmas, which must be the most popular place for men in the hemisphere. The Green Doors in Catalina Square. Tourists only know the square as a market, but it's where nine out of ten laundry-boys have their first sexual experience. I overheard them borrowing the £7 from the chief laundry man.

MARA   Only to have to pay it back on sub-day, I suppose. Yes, everyone knows when they have it. They don't appear to be sick, yet they're not allowed to work in the catering section. A list used to go up in the mess of those who'd caught it; only to be crossed off when cured. As a result, most of the boys didn't report it, and it spread like wildfire. (*Pause*) What do these students know of real life?

FASHSHAR   They'll learn.

MARA   Or dons, for that matter. Bones marrowed out from adolescence by the Oxford tutorial's grinding a-sexuality. Starved of warmth and tight-lipped, fondling neuroses into articles, your mental self-importance into worthless books.

FASHSHAR   You're in a dream.

MARA   If I'm in a dream, history is God's nightmare. No, I'm in the real world.

FASHSHAR   Well, you'll be glad to hear that I've just used my column in *Woman's Eternal* to attack a dozen of my colleagues who've published a book together. It didn't take me long, as I only skimmed and had

read nothing of the person they were writing about.
It's an art. But that will wake them up. I feel as you
do. They've no sense of the outside world.

MARA   But have *you* published anything worth while? That
            people like me could appreciate?

FASHSHAR   No. But that's not the point. You don't have to be
            a carpenter to judge whether the chair you are
            sitting on is good of its kind.

MARA   Is this what you teach your pupils?

FASHSHAR   When I feel like it. I'm blunt; and don't care who
            I offend.

MARA   You are a moral oaf. Here come two of your
            adolescents.

FASHSHAR   Not mine, though I've met them.

MARA   I'm off. (*Exit Mara*)

SCENE   FOUR

Enter Thalassios and Gan.

THALASSIOS Hullo! We tried having Gan dress as a woman to
            woo the lesbian, but it didn't work.

FASHSHAR   Well, there you have it. Crumpet from two very
            different backgrounds. Koinonia secure, a brother
            and a sister, happy suburban home, expects no more
            than to marry and settle in the Home Counties.
            And Amatrix, adopted, insecure, as a result
            ambitious, with neuroses that make her both creative
            and potentially manic-depressive. She has the Cam-
            bridge gloss and professionalism; Koinonia, Oxford's

quieter security and shabby-genteel unselfconsciousness.

GAN   Any generation before now it would have been
               ridiculous to say this, but I think I would rather
               have been born a girl today than a boy.

FASHSHAR   Perhaps Amatrix should have dressed as a man to
               woo you? You'd get on fine with Mara.

GAN   I did take her to dinner once.

FASHSHAR   Oh you did, did you?

GAN   Yes. Never again. I had only just enough money to
               last the term, and carefully ordered a half bottle of
               wine at a pound. Then I asked her out of politeness
               if she liked it. She looked down the wine-list, and
               recognized another she liked costing two pounds
               seventy a half. Then she pretended to have caught
               sight of the price, laughed, and said 'It's all right.
               I'll have the cheap one.' Of course I ordered the
               expensive one. She had entirely controlled the
               decision.

THALASSIOS   What do the Chinese say? 'Disorder is not sent down
               from Heaven, it is produced by women.' (*Wistfully*)
               Yet Mara does make me blush when she smiles.

FASHSHAR   It's because she knows what you have in your pocket.
               Some women want to wear you like a glove; to live
               their lives not with you but through you. Ask
               yourselves whether either of your girls is like that.
               And if so, drop her.

THALASSIOS   (*Together to each other*) There's something about
& GAN   your girl . . .

FASHSHAR   Amatrix's main jealousy is not that Koinonia has
             Thalassios but that Thalassios has Koinonia.

THALASSIOS   But I haven't! I've brought a poem along about
             her, but Amatrix suits the metre better.

GAN   So have I, but Amatrix is too short for mine.

FASHSHAR   I suppose you're going to ask the girls if they want
             their lines endstopped!

THALASSIOS   (*Holds up hand for silence. Reads*)

             Better far the lazy eyes
             Closed in languor at sunrise
             Effortlessly lost in sleep
             Where the scythe can never reap,
             Than the chromium day's despair
             Swept grotesquely here and there.
             Best of all, where joy embalms –
             Soft Amatrix' sensual arms.

FASHSHAR   It's a ridiculous set of lines – but Amatrix fits the
             last line better than Koinonia.

THALASSIOS   And her arms are more obviously sensual. I can't
             think of Koinonia as sensual.

FASHSHAR   I hope yours is better.

GAN   Light-eyed Koinonia's
             Faun-touched hair
             Never so soft
             Never so fair
             Brightness enhances
             Evening and dawn
             Happiness dances
             Rapture is born.

FASHSHAR   Vile! Vile. There's nothing in it. Nothing! Either

in your poem or choice of whose name. Ah well!
Così fan tutte, they're all the same. Why don't you
each swap and woo the other's bird?

THALASSIOS   (*Together*) Would you mind?
& GAN

FASHSHAR   And here they come. Put away your warbling, you'll
never snare chicks like that. I'll leave to shaft Mara.

THALASSIOS   (*Together*) Good luck!
& GAN

Exit Fashshar.

SCENE FIVE

Enter Koinonia and Amatrix.

GAN   Where have you been? We've missed you.

*Amatrix faces Gan, Koinonia faces Thalassios.
Pause. Amatrix and Koinonia change places with
each other at the same time as Gan and Thalassios
change places. They are thus still facing their original
partners. Pause. Then Amatrix addresses Thalassios
and Gan Koinonia.*

AMATRIX   Ah! I see. Unlikes attract, likes repel.

GAN   A near Miss.

THALASSIOS   How was the film?

KOINONIA   Amatrix had three cigarettes, and I had to wake her
for two of them.

AMATRIX   I was tired.

GAN   When I'm too tired, I take an interminable time getting myself to bed. Become over-neat, write up my diary, prepare tomorrow's shirt, shoes, delay . . .

KOINONIA   I hate being ill in the daytime. We had some sunflowers like lions. I 'phoned my aunt, and the operator had a terrible cold and of course I caught it, and the sunflowers smelled like apples.

AMATRIX   I have a fear of being lost. That terrifying poem 'James, James, Morrison, Morrison . . . lost or stolen or strayed . . .'. You know it.

GAN   You should try the jungle.

THALASSIOS Or sea-swimming.

AMATRIX   Why sea-swimming? That's a family sport.

GAN   Never lose faith with brother water. You can always boil it; and it never lets you down.

THALASSIOS Where I come from there's a north breakwater and a south breakwater, and the tide comes slantways in across the bay. That's why there've been so many drownings there. The swimmers fight it, instead of tacking with it like a boat, and letting it bring them in. (*To Gan*) Do you swim?

GAN   With compelling ease.

THALASSIOS Don't you be so sure. There are two wrecks there, sharp as razors. In 1911 no loss of life, by 1914 eleven had died, but since then? Ninety-three! Like a magnet to children. There's you, calling through the megaphone to 'keep away', and the parents are saying 'Leave them be. Boys will be boys!' And the next thing you're doing is washing up the body. You know what the eddy round a wreck is like.

AMATRIX   No?

KOINONIA   I hate death because I love life.

THALASSIOS I'm glad to hear it. I was sitting having a lemonade
            on the pier, just me, and a little chap fishing; and
            his friend – another boy – came running up and said
            'There are two men out there waving for help!' So
            I took off my shirt and shoes and trousers and dived
            in wearing only my underpants. As soon as I'd dived
            in I wished I hadn't. The sea was pounding the
            swell back against the pier in a cycle, and I was in
            the middle of it, so I had to go down-bay half a
            mile in the wrong direction with the tide, to get
            round it. By the time I reached the first man he was
            shouting and panicking. I shouted 'If you'll play
            ball with me, I'll try to save you both!' So he shut
            up, having scratched half my back off, and did what
            I told him and lay on his back. Then I made for
            the second man who was even further out, but by
            the time I reached him he was floating face down-
            wards in the water. If we'd got him ashore there
            and then and given him the kiss of life he would
            still have come back; but we were nearly a mile out
            to sea by now.

AMATRIX   What did you do?

THALASSIOS I pushed one, lying on his back, and pulled the
            corpse by the hair, and got them back to the beach
            where their wives were clearing up the picnic. The
            men should never have gone in. The red flags were
            flying. But the beach was deserted except for the
            boy fishing and myself on the pier, and they thought
            they could risk it. (*Pause*) Do you know, I've never
            heard a word from the man I saved since?

KOINONIA   I suppose it's only natural. How can one repay
            that?

THALASSIOS When my elder brother heard he was very angry.
            'Next time someone asks you to save two drowning

men on your own, just you be in the sauna, on the lavatory. You were damn lucky they didn't pull you down.'

AMATRIX   I think I'd just have prayed.

THALASSIOS   Who knows what God is?

GAN   The informing principle of nature in the created universe. Every scientist will tell you that.

KOINONIA   But what has that to do with love?

GAN   That is love. That's justice!

AMATRIX   God help us.

KOINONIA   Has your jungle-work put you in danger?

GAN   Even driving's a risk. If you run over a black mamba in your jeep and don't kill it, it will loop over until it sinks its fangs into something; and God help you if the windows of your jeep are open.

KOINONIA   I should have thought the animals were afraid of you; unless you run them over, of course!

GAN   As soon as they see you, they instinctively go away. Snake, lion, every wild animal will run on its first encounter with man. But it comes back; and if it meets you then, it attacks.

AMATRIX   It can't all be danger. I'd love the jungle!

KOINONIA   I'm not so sure. Think of a tiger on a dark night.

GAN   It's funny. The white tiger, which should be in Siberia, is in India. All tigers were originally from Siberia. A cold country. But the way they adapted to the heat of India is remarkable. The stripes are because in cold countries they need camouflage in summer in the marsh areas among the reeds.

AMATRIX   I don't believe a word of it!

KOINONIA   Wait a minute! I'm fascinated.

GAN   The tiger makes love all day and hunts all night, whereas the lion mates in the afternoon, and hunts all night and in the morning. When tigers are mating they don't need food. When they're excited they don't eat. They make a great fuss for seven days on end. The first proposal comes from the female. She rubs herself against the male. She walks, or louches ahead of the tiger, and then suddenly makes it easy for the tiger to mount. If he ignores her, then she attempts to copulate exactly as a male would. She comes back again, and rubs her body against him, actually kissing him sometimes, and mounts him. Afterwards she slips out quickly like a bullet from the tiger's hold, turns her face, and delivers a short fight. She hits him first. Then both of them lie flat on the ground, rolling on their bodies, and wave their legs in the air: which is difficult but relaxing. Then, once again, after fifteen minutes they start copulating again.

KOINONIA   It's all too much.

GAN   You should see a charm or ostentation of peacocks!

KOINONIA   No. I learn very slowly. Enough. I feel with St Aldhelm who wrote, 'At last, and by God's grace, after unceasing labour I have mastered that most difficult of all things, what they call fractions.'

THALASSIOS   Come and have a glass of wine.

KOINONIA   Shall we?

AMATRIX   Just for a short while.

KOINONIA   The modest water saw her Lord, and blushed.

GAN   Monod says that according to the laws of chance, the probability of life appearing on this planet is just about nil. Crick and Orgel think we come from directed panspermia – Earth was seeded from outer space.

Exeunt, Broomy entering.

BROOMY   They've gone off with the wrong girls! I don't know what students are coming to these days. Indiscriminate. Like seagulls following a harrow. I'll go to bath with the ducks.

Exit.

SCENE SIX

The six characters sit in pairs, each pair being one point of a triangle: Koinonia and Amatrix, Mara and Fashshar, Gan and Thalassios.

AMATRIX   You know how it is. When you do fall totally in love with someone, they begin to retreat until you are reaching out for them and hopelessly hooked.

KOINONIA   Marriage is an issue of blood.

MARA   You only came back because you don't want to feel that sense of failure rejection brings.

FASHSHAR   If you wait until you are twenty-seven, you'll search the orchard and pick the crab.

GAN   The Mormons go in for baptism of the dead. You have to get your ancestors out of hock, photocopied. The result is a beautiful . . . photocopier.

THALASSIOS   The permafrost of matrimony does not lift.

KOINONIA   What a *nice* man he is! One of God's anointed.

AMATRIX   I'd give anything to find one person in the world who looks like me!

FASHSHAR   Engagement is the gift of a bird singing in its cage.

MARA   And marriage is the discovery that it's artificial.

THALASSIOS   She was over thirty, and insisted on a sperm-count, so I fled.

GAN   If your ex-wife has a baby, are you the step-father?

FASHSHAR   Making love to a woman on the pill is empty. The magic of potential life is not even imaginatively there. The gold of your seed becomes spittle.

AMATRIX   He put his hands in the peas to see if they were hot, and then went off to another table! Some of us had to eat those peas! And you know some of the things men use their hands for.

GAN   Chauvinism? Now there's hemisphereal chauvinism. The South wants the atlas upside-down.

MARA   We gave it a good try. I found the impact of your personality on mine destructive. I've no doubt you find mine even more so on yours. There's no fault. It's the mixture, the chemistry. We are such utterly different people, in every respect: background, outlook, needs, hopes . . . We had to part.

THALASSIOS   Imagine it. The hotel porter comes to you in the foyer and says, 'That girl there says will you love her this evening, now, while your wife's away?' The call of the wild!

KOINONIA   We have to change our names. But have you noticed? It's one of the most consistent and systematic features of angels that they refuse to give their names. You would have power over them if they did. They're ex-directory.

AMATRIX   If you're a woman, you're so much more aware of your body than a man is. Since I was nine, when I began to bud. Then first period, at school, and each cycle of depression, sickness, stomach-ache, even my complexion regularly affected, first hair . . . and men call it moods!

GAN   I really enjoy women. Their moods, their habits, their private rituals, their poses, their cattiness, their hypocrisies, their flirtatiousness, their breasts . . .

FASHSHAR   I went out with you three more times afterwards, but you were cold as a cinder.

THALASSIOS Everyone is taken for someone else. Result? Permanent identity crisis.

KOINONIA   He's not sarky and sly like some people. He's open and straightforward, and very clever as well.

MARA   You could only think of me as someone to go to bed with, not as a friend, as someone to share at least some of your life with.

GAN   According to Mazdean belief, the fire of judgement will be molten torment to sinners, but like warm milk to the righteous.

MARA   You were aggressively sexual.

KOINONIA   A pathetic phallacy.

AMATRIX   A long-standing error.

FASHSHAR   Would you have liked it if I were not? Don't be daft. I know your bodily rhythms and wants. And mental, too. You want to be thought desirable.

THALASSIOS   But say she becomes the sort of wife who leaves the washing-up in the sink?

MARA   Opportunity recedes with time.

KOINONIA   (*Watching Gan as he does it*) I like the way he puts his fingertips and toetips together when he thinks.

THALASSIOS   You're always struggling between Heaven and Hell while I'm trying to work out the practicalities!

FASHSHAR   But you made sex a payment to be earned! Yet needed it yourself just as much, you hypocrite!

GAN   Then after the hotel, back home; to all a wife's welcoming disapproval.

AMATRIX   What about Mara?

KOINONIA   She always looks at you with the whites of her eyes.

THALASSIOS   I suppose adulthood is when you realize that a second-best life is a damn sight better than a third-rate one.

MARA   I don't see it like that. You say you love me, but you only help me when it suits you.

GAN   There must be an enormous sense of relief when your first wife gets married.

AMATRIX   Many couples part after the first adultery, as they love their pride more than their partner.

FASHSHAR   When I drove your luggage to London, and had

finally unloaded everything and unpacked for you, then, and only then, did you give it me.

GAN   Yet if one persists in being a mediator, a go-between, it's not long before one ends up a scapegoat.

THALASSIOS   But culture has been superimposed on instinct, and as marriage is only the minutest portion of genetic time, it's against nature.

MARA   We were busy till then. I need to relax.

FASHSHAR   I'm sorry we can't change the relationship, at least into friendship.

AMATRIX   (*Of Thalassios*) His come-to-bed soft hands!

KOINONIA   (*Of Fashshar*) He's strange. 'Oh, be a fine girl, kiss me right now, sweetheart!' Then that tuft of a beard in your face.

THALASSIOS   I'll marry my boat.

GAN   Marriage is a lie we have agreed upon.

FASHSHAR   So can't we remain friends?

MARA   We never have been.

KOINONIA   C'est la vie.

AMATRIX   C'est la guerre.

               Blackout.

Griot. Enter to him Fashshar.

GRIOT   Fashshar?

FASHSHAR   You sent for me?

GRIOT   How are you feeling?

FASHSHAR   I feel like a sixteen-year-old. (*Pause*) But I can never get one!

GRIOT   I'm afraid there are complaints against you.

FASHSHAR   Oh. I'm on public trial, am I?

GRIOT   Public? The only people present are those you see.

FASHSHAR   I feel like a boy at his headmaster's.

GRIOT   Would you like to sit down?

FASHSHAR   Perhaps I'd better. What's it all about?

GRIOT   I'll go through them with you.

FASHSHAR   Them? Are there several? (*Pause*) Are they against me professionally, or against my private life?

GRIOT   You must judge. But remember, though we are friends, and have been during the short time you've been with us, I am now talking to you as Master of your College.

FASHSHAR   Oh, come off it. This isn't the nineteenth century! I know your weaknesses, you know mine.

GRIOT   Don't make it harder for me.

FASHSHAR   Make what harder for you? Surely I can't be sacked.
            I've been appointed for life.

GRIOT   No one, not even you, has that security. I know
            many of the younger dons think that's the case, but
            it is not. You have to be re-elected every few years,
            and that re-election depends on your not being
            everywhere spoken against; on your carrying the
            goodwill of your colleagues with you.

FASHSHAR   I see. And I'm losing it. What are you driving at?

GRIOT   In good time.

FASHSHAR   Look, what the hell is the matter? If you have
            complaints against me, let me know them. I imagine
            it's something to do with my attacking Faculty
            colleagues? I'm allowed my critical opinions, aren't
            I? That's fair comment. I genuinely do think they
            are a crackbrained lot, and pretty mediocre as
            scholars.

GRIOT   That's not the charge. You've fouled your own nest
            there by pronouncing on their author whom you
            had neither studied nor understood. No. The first
            major charge is from the students about your teach-
            ing.

FASHSHAR   Oh? My politics are not Oxfordian? My tutorials
            begin late, end early, and are often changed?

GRIOT   Your conscience is alert! One case in point is from
            a lady, accepted here to read for a higher degree
            on Gissing, who has asked, after more than a year
            with you, to be transferred, as she knows you still
            know nothing of the subject.

FASHSHAR   I see. But a research supervisor can't be expected
            to keep up with all a research student is doing! His
            job is merely to guide, to be a sounding-board, to
            see the thesis is properly presented . . .

GRIOT   She says you still don't know which characters are in which book. We've transferred her to a senior colleague.

FASHSHAR   Not one of those I've attacked? Look, this is ridiculous!

GRIOT   Listen first, before you lose your temper. I'm giving you the minimum. The next is about your lectures. They report that you lost your temper at the start of one of your lectures and stalked out, leaving one of the more experienced ladies present to take over, so the evening wouldn't be entirely wasted. Oh, you did come back at the end and mumble some sentence of apology, but by then most had left . . .

FASHSHAR   But it was only an evening class!

GRIOT   Exactly. These classes carry what we do to the out-side world. They are our public service; and people, yes, human beings with far less spare time than students, come; and they judge our University by men such as you.

FASHSHAR   Frustrated housewives and retired schoolmasters and coalmen.

GRIOT   And Government Inspectors allocating grants, watching. It seems from yet another series of com-plaints that your examining is perfunctory. You handed back files and essays, on which students had spent two years, in five minutes; much of it clearly unread.

FASHSHAR   Just a minute. I was supposed to correct the written papers. I only glanced at all those files.

GRIOT   That's the complaint. Your predecessors read every word, and spent over an hour with each and every student discussing their work-in-progress face-to-face.

FASHSHAR   Any more?

GRIOT   Only lesser ones. You fail to turn up to committee meetings. They say you only appear when you want to cast a negative vote against one of your enemies.

FASHSHAR   Every time I go, the Chairman welcomes me to the Committee for the first time!

GRIOT   Your blue jokes.

FASHSHAR   You'll make me see red.

GRIOT   Good. You are not inviolate. You can squirm, duck, posture and look back, but these are grave charges, and you are as unpopular as it is safe for someone as insensitive as you are to be.

FASHSHAR   I'll take no more insults.

GRIOT   I've stuck to facts. You may no longer be able to distinguish.

FASHSHAR   I'll leave.

GRIOT   Before you go, one word. What do you think a University is? I'll tell you. It's no more nor less than this: a family of people who love their subjects gathered round those who live their subjects.

FASHSHAR   Oh, slick.

GRIOT   But true. The buildings, libraries, chapels, High Tables, all are trappings. It's a student's choice of subject that brings him to a certain teacher, and mastery of that subject that put the teacher there in the first place.

FASHSHAR   Then I can claim that honour! What rubbish.

GRIOT   You annoy me. I wasn't going to tell you, but now I will. When you were interviewed for your job here, you were bottom of the list of three. You were not liked. But as sometimes happens, the one to whom we offered the post died, and the second on the list had already accepted another by the time we informed him; and it was too late to advertise again if we were to have a don teaching for the coming term. You were a disliked, compromise candidate. And you've done nothing to improve your position since.

FASHSHAR   I've a friend in the youngest Professor.

GRIOT   He tolerates you as his yes-man. You ape his accent. But haven't you noticed? He's never with you when you shout your mouth off in the pub at morning coffee-time.

FASHSHAR   If you were not Master, I'd hit you.

GRIOT   At least this interview has taught you something – that I am.

FASHSHAR   You'll hear more of this, you ridiculous kipper.

GRIOT   I wish to see no more of you. Good night.

          Blackout.

SCENE EIGHT

Light up on Amatrix, sola.

AMATRIX   I feel like a snowman built in the middle of the road overnight, waiting. (*Pause*) Separated from the loved one, blemishes fade and idealization takes over. (*Sighs*) This morning I was waiting for him to knock.

No reason why he should. Silent house. Every foot-step outside, every creak of a board, every beat of the pulse might, might not, be him. No. Learn to discount the possibility. Yet this one might just be him? Discipline! Discount all noise until he actually arrives. It will be clear enough. No. No sign.

Thalassios has entered silently behind her and now suddenly puts his hands over her eyes.

Good God! He's behind me! (*Pause*) I know it's you. I can tell from the perfume you've just come from Koinonia.

THALASSIOS   If she wears beer. Look, she's not a 'How d'ye do?' and hop in the sleeping-bag with you. She's a nice girl with neither bark nor bite; that's why I like her.

AMATRIX   Have you come to tell me that?

THALASSIOS   I just threw out the remark.

AMATRIX   What do you expect me to do? Agree?

THALASSIOS   Just throw it out. You said you'd 'phone.

AMATRIX   The very thought that if I didn't call you would be upset made me not want to call.

THALASSIOS   Are you happy now? Have the hypocrisies been observed?

AMATRIX   It's our last year. Like driving to Heathrow on a spring morning; a sudden love of the valleys and green fields soon to be left behind. Perhaps it's better not to have and to want something, than to have something and no longer want it?

THALASSIOS   A woman may have to become engaged to a man before she discovers she cannot marry him.

AMATRIX   In wooing the man surrenders to the woman, but in marriage it's the other way round, and it lasts longer.

THALASSIOS   You realize how desperately important the stars are when you're sailing alone at sea on a night so dark you can only see the furrow of your boat, and blackness. (*Pause*) You might try to love me.

AMATRIX   The child's honeymoon with life! That's innocence. Waking from the dream of childhood, still to retain that dream.

THALASSIOS   Tides change. Unhappiness can enrich.

AMATRIX   True. It can deepen understanding.

THALASSIOS   Life is soon to become more serious for everyone.

AMATRIX   To live is to love, and to love is to love romantically.

THALASSIOS   Heresy! But at least heresy means choice.

AMATRIX   As women have a shorter flowering-time, they can suffer from decision-fatigue.

THALASSIOS   Bold choices often spring from despair.

AMATRIX   Look! I'll test you, and tell you what I am. You probably have no idea. I'm not a virgin.

THALASSIOS   I don't waste time worrying about virginity.

AMATRIX   At boarding-school you spend hours thinking of nothing else.

THALASSIOS   Have a toffee?

AMATRIX   Toffee? Huh! He was a junkie. I heard this rustling of what I thought was a toffee-paper behind my back as we clinched in the car. A car! I ask you.

Not the place a young girl at boarding-school thinks of for the altar of her virginity. Anyway, at least it was the *front* seat, not sordid on the back seat like in dirty stories. But that's why it wasn't a success. Just up and down. Horrid! I didn't even know it came in tissue-paper. And it's not nice to be told the cost of Durex is exorbitant when you are about to be made a woman for the first time. There it was, precious for years, gone. I felt awful. It meant nothing to him. He never saw me again.

So then there was the 'Business Arrangement'. He at least knew what he was doing. I met him on a train, and was feeling so demoralized after being dropped and having lost my virginity that I thought, 'Oh, it doesn't matter now. Might as well be whoever wants it. Ten or a dozen make no more difference than one. Who knows? Who cares?' So the 'Business Arrangement'. He ignored me in company and smelled of beer. No question of love on either side. Clumsy Sunday afternoons while his girl-friend was abroad. I never dreamt I'd do such a thing! Six months earlier I'd have been sick at the thought. But I had to cheer myself up. Now I've you, I feel sick at the thought of him; though it didn't seem to matter at the time. But I still hate hearing rustling paper when I kiss.

THALASSIOS   I'm not so sure about unhappiness enriching.

AMATRIX   You must know me as I am. I was very young. I'd only met the junkie once, at a party, and I worshipped him. He arrived with his shirt hanging out, late. Everyone else in evening dress. Just saw him that one time. Then nine whole months of 'phone-calls. His father always answered, and said, 'It's disgraceful! You have to spend all your pocket-money in coin-boxes.' (*Laughs*) He was ace! Junkie or no, he'd roar with laughter with his mouth open all red.

Once when I 'phoned he said he'd left fourteen pounds' worth of dope burning on the basin; so I said, 'You'd better finish it.' But he said he'd rather talk to me. That really flattered me! Tiddles the junkie. He was gorgeous when I first met him, but a year later he was rubbish. Couldn't sleep at nights because he could hear his heart beating.

THALASSIOS   And he made you a woman?

AMATRIX   When he put out his hand in the Chinese take-away his nails had blood on them. I didn't know you bled. I didn't even see his body. It was dark. I'd waited and waited to see what a man looked like, and then I never did.

THALASSIOS   But some say you are a lesbian.

AMATRIX   No. I had a boy-friend at Cambridge before I came up. At Trinity. I'd already been to balls, met the Master, Butler, and so on. Yet throughout the whole of my second year I was celibate. You won't believe it; but I was so much more at ease with my own sex, I suppose I could have become one. But I'd have guilt-feelings about not using my undergraduate years to find a partner while the odds are on my side, and there's more male variety than I'll ever have in my life again. So I met this boy and gave him a subscription to *Penthouse* for his birthday, and each month drooled over the spread girls with him. This satisfied him, and satisfied me at the same time, till we were both satisfied. Funny how hard the transition to men is if you've spent all your life at a girls' boarding-school!

THALASSIOS   I knew about your fits of depression and elation; but when you haven't seen someone for a while, and you've been assuming all along your image was the true one, and she will be just the same when you next meet, and she isn't, it's disorientating.

AMATRIX   What is a woman to do? She knows she has fewer
               years than a man. What young man would marry a
               woman over forty? Yet what young woman would
               not marry a sensitive and experienced forty-year-old
               man? It's unfair. But it also means a woman has to
               shop around, and this gives her a bad reputation –
               which *could* be attractive, I suppose! So a beautiful
               woman should be allowed simultaneous lovers,
               whereas a man can afford to set an example of
               constancy.

THALASSIOS   I will, but you are not.

AMATRIX   You have the fixed grin of the totally petrified!
               (*Weeps*)

THALASSIOS   May the healing angel touch
               Your swansdown body with so much
               Pressure as will heal and cure
               With true health that will endure
               As love endures; for body should enjoy
               So richly that no illness can destroy.

AMATRIX   For you my cheeks will be as soft as sheets, hair like
               a pillow's down.

               Exeunt.

                        S C E N E   N I N E

               Enter Broomy.

BROOMY   Ah, there they go! (*Cheerfully*) Students. Nothing
               but a dirty filthy lot, bless them. Dons are no better.
               I came here one morning and found the Senior
               Tutor had committed suicide under my newly-
               planted elder-bush. What had he got against me?
               Give me farmers every time. They know the lie of the
               land. And its truths. They tame the ground until
               the ground tames them.

Enter Fashshar.

How d'ye do, sir. (*Winces*) Oh!

FASHSHAR   Hullo, Broomy! Are you in pain?

BROOMY   Pain's not new to me; although I wish it were.

FASHSHAR   Have you always been in this garden?

BROOMY   Me? No. I was a taxi-driver in the war. Too old to fight. Oh, my legs used to jump about something terrible when I was in bed at nights. Very bad job for the heart. Coronaries, ulcers. You're not out in the air enough, don't get enough exercise. High on adrenalin. You can't take more than five hours; then you have to stop. Now, it's different. I'm out in the open all day, *and* I take time to relax when I get in. I'll never take a taxi again.

FASHSHAR   Do you know Mr Griot?

BROOMY   Oh, I knew his dead wife well. She sacked her gardener for thieving cauliflowers, and three weeks later he was back to her for a reference. 'I'll think about it', she said: and then wrote 'Garsper got more out of my garden than anyone else ever did.' She might as well have put 'He assures me he does not drink'. Ho, ho! Dear old Garsper!

FASHSHAR   No, I mean the Master.

BROOMY   Not been this way, though two young'uns have. Fair trellised together they were. Don't know how they could keep their balance. How's your young Miss? Have you settled your differences yet?

FASHSHAR   Were you ever married?

BROOMY   Yes. I'll never marry again. I had a good one. It's
            sad to see them go.

FASHSHAR   If you're a friend of the Master, and I know he's
            fond of you, would you put in a word for me? I
            lost my temper with him, and want to apologize.

BROOMY   (*Holding out his hand behind his back*) I can't be
            bought, sir. I can't be bought.

FASHSHAR   (*Laughing*) Oh you good friend! (*Pressing coin into
            his palm*)

BROOMY   I'll do what I can. Why have a dog and bark your-
            self? I'll do your rooting.

FASHSHAR   That's the last thing I want! Are you all right?

BROOMY   (*Wincing*) I won't be playing bowls today. I knew
            something was wrong this morning when I was
            watering the grass in the pouring rain.

FASHSHAR   (*Laughing*) Good luck! Make my peace.

BROOMY   Piece of cake.

            Exeunt different ways.

                    S C E N E   T E N

            Gan and Koinonia.

GAN   There is no splendour in the sun
            While you are absent from my arms,
            And though I search till day is done
            Remission in oblivion
            Watching the busy crowd go past,
            Driving the brain, callousing palms,

No high philosophy rings true
Nor can contentment come, till you
Bring peace of mind, and rest at last.

KOINONIA   See ! The light fails on the dark water there.
Put sprigs of secret myrtle in my hair
    For bridal love.
The railway sounds more clear now, comforting,
With the late birds' brisk twitters echoing
    In the still air.
The darkening grass folds up the daisies' heads,
And blackening trees brush children to their beds.

Tie up our toys, for we must face the world.
Please would you put down, where that hedgehog's
    This saucer of milk ?   [curled,
He's my new friend. The sycamore's winged fruit
Will soon be spinning the moth's parachute.
    I'll share your life.
My sleeping breasts will rise for you alone.
Your lips sealed up, my garden is your own.

SCENE ELEVEN

Enter Fashshar and Mara.

FASHSHAR   (*He*) Look back, look back ! (*She*) Not so. (*He*)
& MARA   Why won't you stay ?
            (*She*) What's here to stay for ? (*He*) All my life is
                yours.
            All that's to come. (*She*) The time has passed for play,
            I must away. (*He*) I'll turn to none but whores !
                (*She*) Take whom you will. (*He*) Can you not
                    even grieve ?
                (*She*) We met, we've tried, we've grown apart,
                    must leave.

(*He*) Let me try once more! (*She*) Flowering time is
   brief,
Girls cannot linger, waiting love's return.
(*He*) We can look back and build on more than
   grief!
(*She*) Our freshness has departed, and concern
   For you as much as me makes me depart.
      (*He*) I'll win you back! (*She*) Fool! Do not
      break your heart.

(*He*) What will you do? (*She*) The world has men
   enough.
(*He*) And yet you said adulteries must cease!
(*She*) They must. (*He*) How then? What will you do
   for love?
(*She*) I'll braid my hair, live cross-legged from the
   knees.
      (*He*) Where will you go? (*She*) Where you must
      never seek there:
   I'll live the College Master's new housekeeper.

SCENE   TWELVE

*Enter to them from one side Amatrix and Thalassios,
from the other, Griot.*

AMATRIX

Where have you been? It's now December!

GRIOT

In Christ Church meadows. It was three o'clock.
The sun low behind dirty-white cloud. Clear, almost
spring-like blue sky; open, vast, crossed by rare
wisps. Seagulls flying low and fast, skimming the
high river. Cygnets with clean white tails, mushroom-
brown feathers still mingling with the white. Bare
trees shrieking in a neat row on the far side. The
wind cleaning and tingling my nostrils, combing
the hair, forcing the flood-tide, brisking the cheeks,
driving everything east. One great white barge left

over from Summer, stately and vacant, bobbing in place, moss on its black underbelly's side. And the grass, muddy-green. Even the hump-backed foot-bridge green with moss. Ducks coming to the lapping edge for bread, ungrudgingly swimming on. Pink reflections in the broken water. Deep puddles on the tow-path. (*Pause*) A long, arched bramble all the time being swept and wrenched as it trails in the race, soon to be dislodged and carried away, broken free from its bank. High, sawn-off telegraph-poles standing out, measuring the yearly floods; while behind, far across the meadows, beyond the water-logged brambles and beeches, tiny boys running between goal-posts under the Merton tower.

AMATRIX   But you went to fetch Broomy!

GRIOT   He died an hour ago.

THALASSIOS   Rocks cut the flesh.

GRIOT   He became his garden.

KOINONIA   Sometimes my eyes feel very heavy in my head.

GAN   The dark angel has touched once more.

GRIOT   If we lament a death, life for us must have meaning. We must pick up the fragments of order left behind.

KOINONIA   Listen! It's gone very quiet. Like birdsong early on Christmas morning.

GRIOT   Let the music start and the engagements be announced. Koinonia, will you take your Gan? Amatrix, your Thalassios? The seasons must turn, and three years come to an end.

AMATRIX   (*To Thalassios*) I know it may not work. But I'm going to try to act as though it will.

THALASSIOS   And so I truly promise to love you for ever.

MARA   We are in a game of chess, and I must mate with an unseen king.

GAN   No marriage lasts, but still we must
             Risk in the hope love grows with trust.
             When you are with me, then we shall delight
             In all the gorgeous pleasures of the night.

KOINONIA   I said 'Your lips sealed up'. King Abundance begat Wisdom on Innocence. Even if our lives are as speckled as a lapwing's egg, we'll hatch our brood.

FASHSHAR   Student marriage? You're behaving like a group of irresponsible children! (*Exit*)

GRIOT   The shadow in the brook. Let him go; each of you pooling two unique and individual lives.

             The six move into a stately dance to the music of Pachelbel's Canon. Lights fade to black.

             End.

DANCE

The dance should have a gentle and leisurely quality. In the parts where the movement is walking, this should be sustained stepping in time to the music (2 crotchet counts for each step).

In the step pattern and its variations, the stepping is quicker (1 crotchet count for each step), but the swaying movement is slow (4 crotchet counts for the sway and return). This change in speed should give a feeling of ebb and flow.

The dance is arranged in phrases of 4 bars each.

The music – Canon in D by Pachelbel is written in common time.

Phrase 1 – walk from the position at the end of the play, to place in a circle facing partners. The girls facing clockwise and the men anti-clockwise.

Phrase 2 – make a circular hay. The hay is made by the girls walking round the circle in a clockwise direction and the men in an anti-clockwise direction. They pass each other grasping alternate hands beginning with the right hand to one's partner, thus giving a chain effect.

Phrases
3 & 4 – partners should meet at the end of phrase 2 and stand side by side holding hands. With partner a hay for 3 is made. Each pair walk describing a figure of eight on the floor and interweave with the other two pairs. The last two counts are used to change to a circular formation with backs to the centre and the man standing on his partner's right, still holding her hand.

Phrase 5 – basic step pattern. The pattern is in two parts. In the first part the steps travel in the forward right direction thus expanding the circle. In the second part the same steps are performed but to the backwards left direction, thus contracting the circle. Steps. Beginning with the right foot take 3 steps (1 count for each) and hold for count 4, then sway back onto left foot (2 counts) and forward onto the right foot (2 counts). This is repeated, but backwards, beginning with the left foot.

Phrase 6 — basic step pattern with variation. Do the three steps to forward right. Man does the two swaying movements but smaller so that he can accommodate the girl as she turns on the spot to the right, turning into his left arm, ending side by side, weight on the right foot. The boy's arm is around the girl's shoulders. The girl's right arm is bent so that her right hand clasps her partner's left hand resting on her left shoulder. The second part of this basic step pattern is done keeping this hand-hold but using the swaying steps to resume hands held side by side (by the girl lifting her partner's hand over her head) and to join hands with adjacent people so that all hold hands around the circle.

Phrase 7 — basic step pattern with second variation. Girls progressing to the right by turning to the right as they travel past their partners to re-form hand-held circle. Basic step pattern; but instead of 2 swaying steps the girl initiates a turn to the right by stepping across herself to the right with the left foot. The body keeps turning to the right as the right foot also steps to the right. The step pattern retreating to the left is as in the basic step pattern.

Phrase 8 — exactly as in Phrase 7, progressing past new partner.

Phrase 9 — exactly as in Phrase 7, progressing past new partner.

Phrase 10 — as in Phrase 5, except all hold hands in circle.

Phrase 11 — taking 4 counts, turn in one sustained movement to partner. Use following 4 counts to gesture to partner:

Amatrix and Thalassios – she strokes his cheek with back of her hand.

Koinonia and Gan – face each other and clasp hands drawing them close together by contracting arms.

Mara and Griot – in 3 staccato movements she puts a hand on his shoulder, he touches the hand on his shoulder, he removes the hand to his side, where he keeps hold of her hand.

Phrases

12 & 13   –   make a hay as in Phrases 3 and 4.

Phrase 14   –   lead off from hay to exit; the third couple holding hands loosely, the other two couples holding each other more closely.

The dance may be lengthened by inserting the basic step pattern (as in Phrase 5) in between Phrases 7 and 8 and Phrases 8 and 9.